## JAY COUNTY PUBLIC LIBRARY

# The Strange Case
# of the
# Reluctant Partners

A novel by
## Mark Geller

**HARPER & ROW, PUBLISHERS,** New York
Grand Rapids, Philadelphia, St. Louis, San Francisco
London, Singapore, Sydney, Tokyo, Toronto

Typography by Joyce Hopkins
1 2 3 4 5 6 7 8 9 10
First Edition

Library of Congress Cataloging-in-Publication Data
Geller, Mark.
    The strange case of the reluctant partners: a novel / by Mark Geller.
        p.    cm.
    "A Charlotte Zolotow book."
    Summary: Thomas is dismayed by a seventh-grade English assignment requiring
him and the intelligent and unusual Elaine to write biographies of each other, but
they soon become good friends.
    ISBN 0-06-021972-6 : $      . — ISBN 0-06-021973-4 (lib. bdg.) : $
    [1. Friendship —Fiction.]      I. Title.
PZ7.G279St    1990                                                        89-29409
[Fic] —dc20                                                                CIP
                                                                            AC

*In memory of my parents,*
*William and Thelma Geller,*
*with great love*

**M**rs. Montgomery said that she had a new assignment for us. Mrs. Montgomery is my English teacher. English is the last class of the day.

"It's a different kind of assignment," Mrs. Montgomery said. "You're going to write biographical sketches of each other."

She said we'd have two weeks to complete them. Most of all she wanted to know what was interesting and special about each of us. We'd discover what that was by interviewing each other, spending time together, and visiting each other's homes.

She was concerned, she said, that if it were left to us we'd all write about someone we already knew well. So she'd chosen a partner for each of us. Partners, she said, would write about each other.

My partner was Elaine Moore. When Mrs. Montgomery read it from her list, my heart didn't go soaring.

Oh, man, Elaine Moore," Alan Pettis said. "Elaine Moore, Trible." We were walking home from school. "Trible you got Elaine Moore."

"Say her name a few thousand more times, Pettis," I said.

"God was good to me," Pettis said. "I got Brigette Coates. Brigette Coates, Trible. Brigette Coates—the most attractive girl in the seventh grade. My partner is Brigette Coates."

"It's swell of you not to gloat, Pettis."

"I prayed for Brigette. Didn't you? I prayed I wouldn't get Elaine. Everyone probably did.

"What ran through your mind when you heard you got her? Did you think it was a nightmare? Maybe you could beg Montgomery to get rid of her.

"What do you think she thinks about getting you? She didn't look thrilled. Maybe she'll beg Montgomery to get rid of you."

"She probably wants *you*, Pettis."

"She can't have me. I got Brigette. I'm in heaven. You got Elaine, Trible. You got Elaine Moore."

What's with you?" my father, ripping an onion roll in half, asked at dinner.

"Me?" I said.

3

"Yeah, you. You're not eating."

"I'm not hungry."

"Why aren't you talking, then?"

"I have nothing to say."

My mother said that I'd been in the dumps all afternoon. She said it had something to do with some girl. I'd told her about Elaine when I got home from school.

"Ooooo," my sister said. She's two years older than I am and takes pleasure in tormenting me. "Thomas has a girlfriend."

"What a jerk," I said.

"You too," my sister said.

"What girl?" my father asked.

"Elaine Moore," I said. "I have to write her biography."

"Elaine Moore?" my father said. "Who's Elaine Moore?"

"Elaine Moore," I said. "I've told you about her."

"Remind me," my father said.

"She's quiet," I said.

"Is that a crime?" my father said.

"It's not only that she's quiet," I said. "She's not friendly. She never smiles and hardly talks to anyone."

"Pass the soda," my father said.

"She's always reading," I said. "Some of the books she reads aren't even normal."

"Are you becoming agitated, Thomas?" my mother asked.

"She brought a radio to school once and listened to an opera," I said.

"Your food won't digest properly if you're agitated," my mother said.

"She doesn't care about her appearance," I said. "Her hair is long and stringy. She probably never washes it. She wears the same ripped jeans every day."

"You're a fashion plate yourself," my sister said.

"No one ever met her family," I said. "She keeps them hidden. I have to go to her house. Pettis thinks I might be in danger."

"Poor boy," my sister said.

"Keep quiet," I said.

"You keep quiet," my sister said.

"Delores called this afternoon," my mother told my father while I gave my meanest look to my sister and she gave me hers. "She and Morty are planning a trip to Atlantic City."

Pettis left our table in the lunchroom the next day to see Brigette at hers. He returned with a dreamy expression on his face.

"Be still, my heart," he said, collapsing in his chair.

"Did you propose?" I said.

"Not yet. We made arrangements to interview each other. I have her telephone number in my pocket. It's her personal phone. Her parents aren't going to answer. I have direct access."

"Congratulations," I said.

"You should smell her perfume," Pettis said.

"It must be heavenly."

"She's wearing peach nail polish."

"Peach?" I said.

"Yeah, peach."

"What's peach?"

"Peach is a color. You knew that."

"No, I didn't know it."

"She wears peach nail polish a lot. She wore grape yesterday."

"Grape?"

"Yeah, grape."

"You're pretty observant, Pettis."

"I know. You're jealous."

"Jealous of what?"

"That Brigette is my partner."

"Oh, yeah, you're right, Pettis," I said. "I'm dying of jealousy."

"I know you are," he said.

"I know you know," I said.

"I know you know I know," he said.

He took a bite of his sandwich and asked when I was going to make arrangements with Elaine. He said that everyone else, if I hadn't noticed, was making arrangements. He said he hoped I wasn't waiting for Elaine to come to me because she wouldn't give me the satisfaction.

"Maybe she would. Maybe she wouldn't," I said.

"You're not making arrangements because you're dreading it," he said.

"I am not."

"You are."

"It's no big deal."

"Do it now, then. Elaine is waiting." She

was five or six tables away eating and read-ing. "Go make arrangements if it's no big deal."

I considered it. Then I said, "I'll make arrangements when I'm good and ready, Pettis. It's not your concern. And wipe the egg salad from your lip."

I approached Elaine during recess the next day while she sat by herself against the school-yard fence read-ing. "Hi," I said, but she didn't look up.

"What are you reading?" I said.

"Nothing that would interest you," she said, still not looking up.

"How do you know?" I said.

"If you must know, it's a short story by Tolstoy."

"How is it?"

"Wonderful. You're making it hard to con-centrate."

"Oh, yeah," I said getting peeved. "Well, excuse me. But we have to talk."

Finally she looked up. "Must we really?"

"Yeah, we must really. We're partners. We have to make arrangements to interview each other."

"What a bother."

"That's what I was thinking. What a bother."

"I suppose we have no choice, though."

"No, we have no choice."

"It is an assignment."

"Yeah, it is an assignment."

"We'll do it, then," Elaine said, and went back to reading. I glanced behind me at Pettis and Robert Krauss laughing by the handball court.

"Are we making arrangements or aren't we?" I said.

"Isn't that why you're here?" Elaine said.

"When do you want to meet?"

"I don't know. When do you want to meet?"

"I don't know."

"That's a problem, isn't it?"

9

"Yeah, it's a problem." My patience was gone. "Do you want to know another problem? It's impolite not to look at someone talking to you."

"Is that so?"

"Yeah, it's so."

"I'll have to remember that."

"Yeah, you remember it."

"I'll set aside some time for you after school," Elaine said, turning a page. "Meet me in the library."

I didn't argue. I was eager to put the experience behind me.

I got to the library first. No one was there but the librarian at her desk. I sat at a table in the corner and started making up questions in my notebook.

Elaine arrived about ten minutes later when I was beginning to worry that she wasn't coming. She plunked her backpack on the table, sat across from me, and asked who was doing the first interview.

I said that whatever she wanted was all right with me. She said that that was chivalrous of me.

"What's that supposed to mean?" I said.

"Let's take turns asking each other questions," she said.

That sounded peculiar to me. I said so, and Elaine said that it didn't sound peculiar to her. For the sake of peace, I went along with it.

"Who's asking the first question?" she asked.

"You can if you want," I said.

"How chivalrous," she said again.

I ignored that and, consulting my notebook, asked where she was born.

"Schenectady," she said. Her elbow was on the table and her chin in her hand. "Where were you born?"

"Schenectady," I said. "Have you ever lived anywhere else?"

"No," she said. "Have you ever lived anywhere else?"

"No," I said. "How big is your family?"

"My parents and me. How big is yours?"

"My parents and sister and me. Aren't you writing any of this down?"

"No. Aren't you writing any of it down?"

"I am," I said.

"Oh, yes, you are," Elaine said and smiled. "It escaped my attention."

"Very funny," I said. "What does your father do?"

"He works for the C.I.A."

"No he doesn't."

"He works for the A.S.P.C.A."

"No he doesn't."

"He's a poet."

"No he isn't."

"It is a matter of opinion, I suppose."

"I'm going to ask him," I said.

"Oh, no. Please don't," Elaine said, leaning back in her chair pretending to be alarmed.

"I have to go to your house to meet your family, remember?"

"Now I do. How could I have forgotten? When are you going to come?"

"When can I?"

"Tomorrow," Elaine said. "I'll take you home with me after school. Why prolong the awful wait?" She got up, slung her back-pack over her shoulder, and started away. "You'll ask gently, won't you?" she said from the doorway. "Oh, please be gentle."

**P**ettis called that night wanting to know all about Elaine. "Was she weird or was she weird?" he asked.

"She was weird," I said.

"I knew it," Pettis said. "What did she tell you about herself?"

"She hardly told me anything."

"You said she was weird. She had to tell you something. What did she tell you about herself that was weird?"

"Nothing," I said. "It was the way she acted."

"How did she act? I have to know. Krauss is expecting me to report to him."

"She was . . . she was sarcastic," I said.

"Sarcastic? How? What did she say? What

did she do? You have to tell me. You can't keep it all to yourself."

"Her father is a poet," I thought to say.

"A poet?"

"That's what she told me."

"A poet," Pettis said. "A poet. Oh, man, a poet."

"I'm going to her house tomorrow."

"I'm going to Brigette's house. I'm sorry. I'm not trying to rub it in. A poet. What would you expect? Her father is a poet."

A re you coming?" Elaine asked as though she couldn't care less at the end of school the next day.

"Yeah, I'm coming," I grumbled.

As we started for her house, keeping a few feet apart, Pettis and Brigette started in a different direction for Brigette's house. Pettis waved at me over his shoulder and grinned.

"Was it difficult sleeping last night?" Elaine asked.

"What do you mean?"

"Did you stay awake excited about coming to my house?"

"Yeah, I was never so excited."

As we walked, I thought about Brigette. She'd worn a purple blouse to school and Pettis had told me to notice how it brought out the color in her eyes. I'd gotten close to her once or twice and was pretty taken with her perfume myself. I held the door for her on the way to French and she smiled at me.

"Hello, Elaine," a black man sitting on a porch said when we'd turned a corner.

"Hello, Aaron," Elaine said.

"Who's that young man you're taking home with you, Elaine?"

"I really don't know, Aaron," Elaine said. "He attached himself to me."

Elaine's house was small, like all the others in the neighborhood. It needed painting and the porch steps creaked. It wasn't too neat inside. The furniture seemed old.

"Wait here and don't steal anything," Elaine said, and went upstairs. I stayed near the front door. A moment later Elaine said, "Yoo-hoo, you can come up now," and I climbed the stairs and followed her to her room.

It was small and cluttered. Elaine sat on the floor with her back against the bed and told me to sit wherever I wanted. I sat on the floor with my back against the wall.

"We're here," Elaine said.

"Yeah, we're here."

"You don't look altogether comfortable."

"I'm fine."

"Jules is busy at his desk. He told me to say hello and that he's looking forward to meeting you. God knows why." She drew her knees to her chest and wrapped her

16

arms around them. "Shall we resume the interviews?"

"It's all right with me."

"Shall I interview you first?"

"If you want."

"How chivalrous."

"If you're going to start—"

"Where were you born?" Elaine asked smiling.

"You know that."

"How big is your family?"

"You know that."

"When are you going to stop twirling your hair?"

"What?"

"You do, you know. You twirl your hair in school all the time. It's a disagreeable habit. It isn't a sign of a placid person.

"You ought to do something about it, Thomas. Have you considered meditation?" I was embarrassed and angry. "I'll show you how. Tuck your legs—"

"Maybe you should meditate yourself."

"I do. Tuck—"

"It's not doing much good, is it?"

"Excuse me?" Elaine said.

"You bite your nails. You bite them in school all the time. It's not a sign of a placid person. It's a disagreeable habit and your nails don't look good."

"Did you say you were leaving?" Elaine said, standing.

"Try polish," I said, standing too.

"Try keeping your advice to yourself," Elaine said.

"Peach is a good color," I said on my way from the room. "So is grape."

I was almost at the front door when it opened. A woman with brown hair, wearing a skirt and blouse, came into the house and smiled at me.

"Hello," she said.

"Hello," I said.

"You must be Thomas. My name is Diane. I'm Elaine's mother. You're not leaving already, are you, Thomas?"

I told her I was.

"I thought you were staying longer," she said. "Didn't you come to meet our family?"

"Something came up," I said.

"I'm disappointed. Will you come another day?"

"Yeah."

"Will you come tomorrow?"

"Tomorrow? I—"

"Didn't you tell me you were busy tomorrow?"

Elaine said that. We looked up at her a few steps from the top stair.

"Yeah," I said. "I have to do errands."

"Come after you've finished your errands," Elaine's mother said. "Come for dinner."

What could I say? If I said I couldn't come, she'd only invite me for another day. I looked up at Elaine again. She glared at me.

"All right," I told her mother.

"Good," her mother said. I heard Elaine run up the stairs. "We'll expect you tomorrow for dinner."

I walked in the door and my mother asked why I was home so soon. I grunted and went to my room. My mother followed me and asked, as I threw myself on my bed, if something had happened.

"Elaine insulted me," I said.

"How did she insult you?"

"She . . . I don't want to discuss it."

"Tell me, Thomas."

"She said I twirl my hair."

"And?"

"She said it wasn't a sign of a placid person."

"And?"

"That's it."

"Thomas," my mother said, "I've heard worse insults."

"I don't like to be insulted at all," I said.

"How did you respond?" my mother asked.

"I insulted her back."

"You didn't."

"I did."

"You know better than that, Thomas."

"No, I don't."

"What did you say to her?"

"It wasn't anything terrible." I wasn't sure any longer I should've said it.

"What did you say, Thomas?"

"I told her that her nails didn't look good. She bites them. I told her to use polish."

"Oh, Thomas, how could you?" my mother said. "You must've hurt her."

"She hurt me," I said.

"Thomas, I want you to apologize."

"No."

"I want you to apologize."

"When she apologizes to me."

"Thomas—"

"I have to go back to her house tomorrow," I said. "Her mother invited me for dinner. I couldn't get out of it."

"I'm glad. It will be a chance to make amends," my mother said. "And Thomas. You really should do something about twirling your hair."

It wasn't a surprise that Pettis called that night. He was more than a little excited about spending the afternoon with Brigette.

"You should see her house," he said. "It's got about fourteen rooms. There's a swimming pool in the back. Her mother took me on a tour.

"Her mother is gorgeous. I swear to God. She doesn't look like somebody's mother. She's got blond hair and a great figure and a great tan. She was wearing shorts. She'd just gotten back from the club.

"They belong to this country club. Brigette's father is this big executive. He's got a Porsche. I saw it in the driveway. He's got a couple of other cars.

"Brigette is getting a car as soon as she turns sixteen. She can choose the car she wants. It doesn't matter what it costs. I swear to God. Her father promised her.

"Her father is pretty handsome himself. He gave me this firm handshake when he got home and made himself a drink. They

22

have this bar in the living room. It was like in the movies.

"What a day. I'm telling you. How was your day with Elaine?"

"I don't want to talk about it," I said.

"Oh, man. Was it that bad?"

"I said I don't want to talk about it."

"I feel sorry for you."

"I have to go, Pettis."

"Brigette took me to her room. Did I tell you that? She's got a stereo and a television and a VCR. She's got all her makeup lined up on her bureau."

Elaine and I sneered at each other once or twice in school the next day but didn't have anything to say to each other. I walked home glum when I should've been happy about the start of the weekend. I stayed in my room until it was time to go to Elaine's house.

"I'm leaving," I called out from the front door.

"Wait," my mother said, and came hurrying from her bedroom. "Let me look at you. Is that how you're going?".

"What's wrong?" I said.

"You've been wearing those clothes all day. Put on something fresh."

"I'm comfortable in these clothes."

"Thomas, go change."

I went to my room, changed my shirt, and returned. My father and sister had joined my mother.

"Satisfied?" I said.

"You look handsome," my mother said.

"Handsome? Thomas?" my sister said.

"Watch your table manners," my mother said.

"I will."

"Change that gloomy expression."

"I can't."

"Are you sure you don't want your father to drive you?"

"I'm not in a hurry to get there."

"Let me drive you," my father said. "You said it wasn't a good neighborhood."

"I hope I'm abducted," I said.

"Thomas," my mother began, "remember to ask if Elaine—"

"I will. Can I go now?"

"You may," my mother said, opening the door for me.

"Have a marvelous time, Thomas, dear," my sister said as I stepped outside.

Hands dug in my pockets, I shuffled to Elaine's house. Everyone I saw seemed carefree and content. No one abducted me.

Elaine's mother greeted me at the door, told me I was very punctual, and introduced me to the man beside her. "Jules, this is Thomas. Thomas, this is Jules. Jules is Elaine's father."

He was tall and lean with a bony face and a friendly smile. His hair was gray and tied in a ponytail. He was wearing tan pants and a blue work shirt.

We shook hands and said we were glad to meet each other. He said that Elaine had been speaking of nothing but my coming. I didn't know what to make of it.

"Elaine, Thomas is here," her mother shouted up the stairs as we went to the living room. I sat on an easy chair and Elaine's parents sat on the couch.

"Did you finish all your chores, Thomas?" Elaine's mother asked.

"What? Oh, yeah. Most of them."

"What chores were they?" Elaine's father asked.

"You know. This and that."

Elaine came bounding down the stairs, sat in the chair across from me, her leg hung over the side, and scowled.

"Did you ask?" she asked me.

"Ask what?" I said.

"Don't you remember? You have a question for Jules. Go ahead and ask him."

Elaine's father asked what it was I wanted to know and I asked if he was a poet. He smiled and I said I knew now that he was and I only doubted it for a minute when Elaine told me because it was an unusual profession.

"Do you like poetry, Thomas?" Elaine's mother asked.

"Yes," I said, not wanting to offend anyone.

"You attend poetry recitals on weekends, don't you?" Elaine said.

"I like 'Lord Randal' and 'Sir Patric Spens,'" I said, pleased with myself for remembering them. "We read them in English last year. I like that poem by Robert Frost about making a decision in the woods, too."

"I thought you'd be partial to limericks," Elaine said.

"Limericks? I like them," I said. Elaine rolled her eyes. Her parents smiled. "I've heard some good ones. I never heard one as good as 'Sir Patric Spens' or 'Lord Randal' or that poem about making a decision in the woods though."

We had potato-and-cabbage casserole for dinner. Elaine's father prepared it. I didn't like the looks of it but it wasn't terrible.

"It's very good," I said.

"Thank you," Elaine's father said.

Elaine said, with disdain, that I brought salami and bologna sandwiches to school. I looked at her parents, wondering what was wrong with that.

"Elaine is a vegetarian," her father said.

"So are you and so is Diane," Elaine said.

"Yes," her father said. "But we're not so intolerant of those who aren't."

Elaine's mother told us about her day. She's a social worker for an agency that helps troubled families.

Then Elaine's father brought up a book he was reading that Elaine and her mother had already read. Her mother liked it a lot. Elaine found it pedestrian.

"I'm reading a book," I said, to get myself back into the conversation.

"Tell us about it," Elaine's father said.

"It's called, *Creatures from the Center of the*

*Earth*. It's about creatures that live in the center of the earth." Elaine rolled her eyes again. "They have an advanced civilization and dominion over the other creatures down there. But they reproduce fast and they're running out of room. So they come to the surface disguised as humans to infiltrate the government and take over the planet."

Elaine's father asked what happened then and I told him that that was as far as I'd gotten. He said he liked science fiction and I said that I did, too, and that I liked Sherlock Holmes mysteries.

"You do?" Elaine's mother said. "So does Elaine."

"I read them over and over," I said.

"Elaine does, too," her mother said.

"My favorite novel is *The Valley of Fear,*" I said. "My favorite short story is 'The Man with the Twisted Lip.'"

"Oh, Elaine," her mother said. "Don't you always say 'The Man with the Twisted Lip' is one of your favorites?"

"Yes," Elaine said softly.

"Did you guess the ending?" I asked.

"I don't remember," Elaine said. "It's been so long since I first read it."

"Same here," I said.

"Listen everyone," Elaine's father said. "I've composed a limerick for the occasion.

*A mystery writer from Napoli*
*Fed her darling son only broccoli*
*And so on. And so on.*
*And so on. And so on.*
*(I'll work on those lines)*
*Then complained that the poor boy was colicky."*

When dinner was ending, her mother suggested that Elaine show me her collection of Sherlock Holmes books. Her father said that he thought that was a good idea.

"He probably doesn't want to see them," Elaine said.

"Yes I do," I said.

"Oh, all right. Come with me," Elaine said, and took me to her room.

There were twenty or thirty Sherlock Holmes books, all in a row, on a shelf above the desk. There weren't only the mysteries but books that analyzed them. There was a book of Sherlock Holmes trivia and a book of Sherlock Holmes quotations.

I said I was surprised I hadn't seen them the first time I was in the room. Elaine smiled and said that I hadn't stayed long.

"I didn't know there were so many Sherlock Holmes books," I said. "I only have a few."

"You can borrow one," Elaine said.

"Really?"

"Go ahead. Give it back whenever you want."

I took the book of quotations.

"Thanks," I said.

"You're welcome," Elaine said.

We went downstairs and chatted with her parents some more. When it was time to leave, and her parents had told me how much they enjoyed my company, she walked me to the front door.

"I had a nice time," I said.

"You did?" Elaine said, with the beginning of a smile on her face.

"Your parents are nice," I said.

Elaine's smile got bigger before it went away and she said, "That's magnanimous of you, Thomas."

"It's what?"

"Magnanimous, Thomas. Magnanimous. You really must do something about your vocabulary."

"My mother wants you to come for dinner," I said. "Can you come tomorrow?"

Elaine stared at me, then left to speak to her parents. "Yes, I can come," she said when she returned.

"Come about five," I said.

"Yes, captain."

I told her my address. "It's about a fifteen-minute walk. Maybe your parents can drive you."

"We don't have a car."

"Oh."

"Good-bye, Thomas," Elaine said, opening the door.

"Good-bye," I said, stepping through it. "I'll see you tomorrow."

# H

ow did it go?" my mother asked when I got home. She and my father were in the living room.

"Not that bad," I said.

"You survived?"

"Yeah."

"What's that in your hand?" my father asked.

"This?" I said. "It's a book."

"I see that it's a book," he said. "What book?"

"A Sherlock Holmes book."

"Did you buy it?"

"Elaine loaned it to me."

My parents looked at each other. I started for my room.

"Is Elaine coming tomorrow?" my mother called after me.

"Yeah, she's coming," I called back.

I lay on my bed, propped the pillow beneath my head, and read a page of the book. Then I put it aside and tried to remember Elaine's father's limerick.

Why can't we have roast beef?" my sister asked my mother. "We always have roast beef when we're having company."

"You know why we can't have roast beef," I said.

"I hate spaghetti," my sister said.

"You do not," I said.

"I'm not in the mood for it," my sister said.

"Too bad," I said.

The three of us were in the kitchen. It was late the next afternoon. My mother was making a salad and my sister and I weren't doing anything.

"Jennifer better not embarrass me," I said.

My sister put her hands on her hips. "Me? Embarrass you? That'll be the day. You're the one always embarrassing me."

"When do I embarrass you?" I said.

"When do you embarrass me?" my sister said. "You embarrass me whenever you bring your stupid friends around when my friends are here."

34

"My friends aren't stupid," I said.

"Excuse me," my sister said. "Who's the one—"

"Beside Krauss," I said. "None of the rest of them are stupid."

My sister asked why I was so worried about the impression I was going to make on someone I didn't even like. I said if I wanted to worry about the impression I made, I'd worry without asking her permission.

My mother sighed and said, "Why don't you two go do something. It's a small kitchen."

"At least I haven't stayed in the house all day," my sister said.

"Visit Pettis," my mother told me.

"I don't feel like it," I said.

"Pettis," my sister said. "There's another—"

"Shut up," I said.

"I'm warning you two," my mother said.

"Leave your mother be," my father shouted from the living room, where he was reading the newspaper.

"Which china are we using?" I asked.

"The good china," my mother said, peeling a cucumber. "And the good silverware."

"You don't think that's too ostentatious?" I said.

"No, it's not ostentatious," my mother said.

"What about meat sauce?" my sister said. "Can't we at least have meat sauce?"

I opened the door for Elaine. She was wearing gray pants and a white blouse. Her hair was pulled back in a braid.

I introduced her to my parents and sister and we sat in the living room. Elaine acted sociable and self-assured.

During dinner my father said he heard that she was interested in opera. Elaine mentioned some of her favorites and my parents tried to remember the opera they'd seen about twenty years ago.

*"Die Fledermaus,"* my father said. "That was

it. *Die Fledermaus*. We enjoyed ourselves, didn't we?"

After dinner, back in the living room, my sister asked Elaine if she sat near me in school. Elaine said she did in art and social studies and my sister asked why she didn't have her seat changed. Elaine smiled and said that sitting near me wasn't so bad at all.

When my sister said she liked Elaine's string bracelet, Elaine said she'd made it herself, took it from her wrist, and told my sister that she could have it. My sister wouldn't take it until Elaine said that she had others and that they were easy to make and that she'd show her how.

Later my sister took Elaine to see her room.

"What a lovely girl," my mother said.

"She's so intelligent," my father said.

"And so attractive," my mother said.

"Elaine?" I said.

"Yes. I love her looks," my mother said.

I stared at Elaine when she returned with my sister. She did look attractive. She saw me staring and I looked away.

When it was time for her to go home, my father insisted on driving her. I waited in front of the house with her while my father got the car from the garage.

"Thanks for coming," I said.

"Thanks for having me."

I made sure no one was on the porch listening.

"Are you busy tomorrow?" I asked.

"No."

"Do you want to do something together? We could go to a movie or something."

"That would be nice," Elaine said, smiling. "I think I'd enjoy a movie."

Pettis called in the morning to ask if I wanted to get together. I told him I had plans. "What plans?" he asked, but I wouldn't tell him.

It embarrassed me, but I told my parents what I was doing and they seemed pleased. I didn't tell my sister—why invite abuse?—and told my parents not to tell her.

I was combing my hair in the mirror above my bureau, getting ready to go, when my sister came into my room. She watched awhile and then asked, "Is that going to take all day or all day and night?"

"All day and night," I said and kept combing.

"Where are you going?" she asked.

"A movie."

"What movie?"

"I don't know."

"Who's going with you?"

"Pettis."

"You're grooming yourself for Pettis?"

"Yeah, I'm grooming myself for Pettis."

She watched me comb a moment more and said, "Well, have a good time."

"Thanks a lot," I said.

"Tell me about the movie when you get home."

"Yeah, sure."

"And tell Pettis . . ." I saw her smile in

the mirror. She's not stupid or anything. "Tell Pettis," she said, and started from the room, "that I enjoyed her visit last night."

Elaine and I had arranged to meet at a bus stop halfway between our houses. She came a few minutes after me, and at the same time the bus arrived.

"No regrets?" she said as we got on board.

"No regrets about what?"

"No regrets about spending the day with me?"

"No." I wished she'd kept her hair in a braid. "No regrets."

We sat toward the back. I mentioned that I hadn't been on a bus in a long time. Elaine said that that was because my parents owned a car. I asked why her parents didn't and she said that they didn't believe in them.

"People die in cars," she said.

"People die all kinds of ways," I said.

"Cars are ecologically disastrous and aesthetically offensive."

I let it go at that and asked if she'd chosen a movie. She said that she had—a French movie.

"What's wrong?" she said, probably because of the way I looked at her.

"Nothing."

"You told me to choose."

"I know."

"Oh, Thomas," she said. "It's not *that* kind of French movie."

I stared out the window. Who'd have believed it? Here I was, when I should've been riding bikes with Pettis or something, going to a French movie with Elaine Moore.

"Jules has taken to writing limericks," Elaine said. "He liked you."

"He did?"

"So did Diane."

"When everyone was talking about books and everything, I was worried that I might've seemed—you know."

"Shallow?" Elaine said.

"Yeah. Why? Did someone say I was shallow or something?"

41

"Jules and Diane," Elaine said, "found you endearing."

"Endearing," I said. "That's what they said? They said I was endearing?"

"In so many words," Elaine said.

The bus stopped and a woman got on. I wondered whether I should resent being called endearing.

"What did your parents think of me?" Elaine asked.

"They thought you were all right."

"Did they say anything specific?"

"My mother thought you were intelligent."

"What else?"

"Let me see. No, that was it. Nobody said you were pretentious or anything."

The movie theater was downtown someplace. It was old and seedy. A woman with a beehive hairdo and glasses on a chain around her neck sold us tickets, and a tiny hundred-year-old usher in a red jacket took them from us.

There were only about ten of us in the audience. All during the movie a woman in the last row complained about being cold. The hundred-year-old usher kept telling her he couldn't do anything about it.

The woman complaining interested me more than the movie. I took three slow trips to the candy counter and, after the first, didn't bother to read the subtitles anymore.

"What did you think?" Elaine asked as we left the theater.

"It was all right,"

"The way you fidgeted—"

"I always fidget. It's a family trait."

We crossed a street.

"I found the story somewhat implausible," Elaine said. "Did you?"

"Not that implausible," I said.

"It was disturbing, though, wasn't it?"

"Yeah, it was pretty disturbing."

I hadn't paid enough attention to know if the story was plausible or disturbing.

"What about those sisters," Elaine said.

"What about them?" I hadn't been aware of any sisters.

"Weren't they evil?"

"Yeah."

"Which did you think was more evil?"

"Which did you think?"

"Oh, the older one. I couldn't stand her. I couldn't stand that priest either. I knew he had to be an imposter. He was so insensitive. How could he speak that way to someone with a tumor in her brain?"

"I don't know."

"Why did the younger sister agree to marry him? Didn't she care that he was the older sister's former husband? Why did they invite those creatures from the center of the earth to the wedding? I knew they'd make nuisances of themselves. Weren't they good dancers though?"

I looked at Elaine and she looked at me and smiled. I told her I hoped she'd enjoyed that. She said she had and thanked me for the opportunity.

I was hungry despite all the candy, and Elaine said she'd be satisfied with a milk shake, so we went to McDonald's. Elaine complained about the smell of the place and I said that the movie theater smelled worse.

She complained about the milk shake, too, and about the french fry I gave her. I tried the milk shake and thought it was fine and thought the french fries were fine. She said that my palate needed remedial attention.

I was beginning a second cheeseburger when her eyes got wide and her straw fell from her mouth.

"Look," she said. "That man by the window. No, don't look. I mean, don't be so obvious. Doesn't that man remind you of something?"

"No."

"Think, Thomas. A Sherlock Holmes story. Doesn't he—"

" 'The Red-headed League,' " I said too loud.

"Shh," Elaine said. "Don't stare."

I said that I'd never seen anyone with such red hair. Elaine said to look at his freckles— he had a few million.

"I wonder if he likes it," I said.

"I wonder if anyone takes him seriously," Elaine said.

"Ask him," I said.

"You ask," Elaine said.

"You saw him first," I said.

"Asking is your idea," Elaine said.

"Do you really want me to ask?" I said.

"Yes, I want you to ask."

"Do you dare me to ask?"

"I dare you to ask."

"I'm going to ask," I said.

"Go ahead. Ask," Elaine said.

I got up. "Don't try to stop me."

"Who's trying to stop you?"

"My mind is made up."

"I know. You're resolute."

I sat down.

"Well," Elaine said.

"Well, what?"

"Are you going to ask?"

"Yeah, I'm going to ask. Let me finish my cheeseburger first. Anyway, what was the question?"

46

After McDonald's we took a walk. We talked about school and Sherlock Holmes and laughed about the man with red hair.

We didn't talk a lot during the bus ride home. I was tired and content. I could tell that Elaine was tired and content, too.

Once when the bus went over a bump we were both lifted out of our seats. We looked at each other and smiled.

We got off the bus where we got on.

"So long, Thomas," Elaine said.

"So long," I said.

"Don't dream about evil sisters."

"I won't. It was a nice day, wasn't it, Elaine?"

"It was, Thomas. I'll see you in school tomorrow."

I began to worry. I worried all the way home. I told my parents that Elaine and I had a pretty good time, went to my room, lay on my bed and kept worrying.

"I'll see you in school tomorrow." Elaine saying that is what got me worried.

I worried what would happen when everyone saw Elaine and me being friendly to each other. I imagined everyone staring at us and asking Pettis what had come over me and laughing and snickering at my expense.

I worried during dinner and almost until it was time to go to sleep. Then it occurred to me that there might not be any reason to worry.

No one would be surprised to see Elaine and me talking to each other. We had to write each other's biography. How could we do it without talking?

We could even be friendly to each other. As long as we weren't too friendly, and we were discreet about what we said to each other when someone was around—I thought of suggesting it to Elaine—no one would think anything of it.

Elaine was at her desk reading when I got to homeroom the next morning. She looked up at me, and barely nodding at her, I went to my desk.

I spent homeroom chatting with Pettis and Krauss and glancing at Elaine. Once I saw her glance at me.

I ignored her all morning and she ignored me. I entered the lunchroom with Pettis at my side.

"When are you going to tell me more about Elaine?" he said. "You've been pretty secretive. I'm hungry for information. Krauss is also. Haven't I been telling you all about Brigette—Where are you going?"

I was on my way to Elaine. She was at a

49

table by herself. I'd decided that I'd rather be with her than Pettis.

"Hello," I said, sitting down.

"Hello."

"You don't mind my company, do you?"

"I suppose I'll tolerate it. I thought you were avoiding me."

"Why would I do that?" I said.

"Because— Never mind," Elaine said.

I was about to take my lunch from my lunch bag when I stopped. "I have a salami sandwich," I said.

"What else is new," Elaine said. "I have a tomato and cucumber sandwich."

"What else is new," I said, and Elaine smiled.

When lunch was almost through I asked Elaine if she was doing anything that afternoon. She said she wasn't and I asked if she wanted to get together.

"We could take a walk or something," I said.

"Sure," Elaine said. "I could probably tolerate that, too."

We took our walk around Elaine's neighborhood. I hurried to her house after hurrying home, leaving off my books, and telling my mother where I was going.

I asked, when we'd been walking a few minutes, how long her father had been a poet. She said since he was a young man and I asked if he ever got anything published.

"Now and then."

"Does he make a lot of money?"

"No."

"Does your mother make a lot of money?"

"Not a lot."

"Does that bother you? I mean, if you had more money, you could probably afford a nicer house in a better neighborhood—"

"I like my house," Elaine said.

"I know. It's a nice house. But it's pretty small—"

"I like my neighborhood."

"Yeah, it's a nice neighborhood—"

"You know, Thomas. There are more im-

51

portant things than big houses in snooty neighborhoods."

"I know. I know," I said.

We walked some more and Elaine said, "Pettis is your best friend, isn't he?"

"I guess so," I said.

"Did he ask why you sat with me in the lunchroom?"

"Yeah, he asked."

"What did you tell him?"

"I told him that I was in the mood for a change."

"What did he say?"

"I don't know," I said. "Half the time I don't listen to him."

Elaine and I took a walk the next day after school, too. She took me to a park near her house.

"Those are geraniums," she said pointing to some red flowers. "The orange flowers are daylilies."

"I don't know much about flowers," I said.

"Why not? It's all right for boys to know about flowers, you know."

"Who said it wasn't?"

We sat beneath a tree. A man and a woman holding hands walked by us.

"It's nice here," I said.

"It's peaceful. I come here to read."

"Only my sister coming could ruin it."

Elaine said that she liked my sister and I said that that was because she wasn't her sister. Elaine said that she wouldn't mind having a brother or a sister.

"Why, is it lonely or something without one?" I asked.

"Yes," Elaine said. "Sometimes I'm lonely."

A while later I was on my back, hands clasped behind my neck, staring at the sky. Elaine was behind me sitting against the tree.

"Elaine," I said.

"Yes."

"You should wear your hair in a braid more often."

"Should I?"

"You look good that way. I know you'll

say that looks aren't important. But if a person looks good wearing her hair a particular way, I don't see why she shouldn't keep wearing it that way."

Elaine didn't say anything. A breeze blew over me.

"Elaine," I said, "do you want to start walking again?"

"All right, Thomas."

"I want you," I said, getting up, "to teach me some more about flowers."

On Friday Elaine and I took another walk around her neighborhood. She seemed out of sorts, so I asked if something was the matter.

"No," she said.

"Are you sure?"

"I told you. Nothing's the matter."

A moment later she asked why I hadn't

sat with her that day or the day before in the lunchroom. I told her I'd sat with her twice that week and wanted to sit with Pettis.

"Have you told him about us getting together after school?"

"No."

"Have you told him that we went to the movies?"

"No."

"Why don't we ever walk in your neighborhood?"

"I don't know."

"I know," Elaine said.

"You do?" I said, annoyed at the interrogation. "Well, let's hear it, then. Why don't we ever walk in my neighborhood?"

"You're afraid," Elaine said.

"Afraid of what?"

"You're afraid that Pettis or one of your other friends will see us."

"I am not," I said, not telling the truth.

"You are."

"I'm not."

"You'd be embarrassed."

"I wouldn't. Everyone has seen me with you in school, anyway."

"It's one thing to be seen in school with Elaine Moore when you have work to do together. It's something else—"

"Maybe it is," I said. "That's because no one has a high opinion of you."

"Oh, no?" Elaine said.

"Why should anyone have a high opinion of you? You don't speak to anyone. You hardly ever smile. You're always read-ing—"

Elaine had turned and hurried in the di-rection from which we'd come.

"Where are you going?" I said, chasing after her.

"Home."

"Why?"

"That's where I want to go."

"I'm sorry, Elaine."

"Don't apologize."

"I didn't mean to upset you."

Elaine stopped and I stopped with her. Her face was red.

"Do you think I have a high opinion of them?" she said.

"You don't?"

"I don't. I have contempt for them. I'll

speak to them as little as I want. I'll smile as little as I want. I'll read when I want. Being friends with them is a small matter in my life."

Then she was on her way again. I followed and kept apologizing. When we reached her house, and she started up the porch steps, I asked if she wanted to get together again.

"I don't know," she said not looking back.

"What about tomorrow? Do you want to get together tomorrow?"

"I don't know."

"Think about it, all right, Elaine?" I said as she opened the door. "I'll call later to find out."

When I got home, my mother asked why I looked so forlorn. I told her I was just tired. Then she said that Pettis had called and wanted me to call him.

I called, sitting on my bed. "Pettis," I said,

57

"I don't want to hear any more questions about Elaine. Do you understand? When I want to tell you more—"

"I didn't call about Elaine."

"I don't want to hear any more about Brigette either. I don't care if she's replenishing her wardrobe. I don't care—"

"She wants you and me to come to her house tomorrow."

"What?"

"She invited me and you to her house. She invited a couple of girls, too. We're going to swim in her pool and have lunch. It was a spur-of-the-moment idea. She thinks you're cute."

"No, she doesn't," I said.

"She does. She told me. We have a pretty intimate relationship. She told me she thinks you're cute."

"She didn't."

"She did."

"She didn't."

"She did. I swear. Where's my Bible? She did."

"What were her exact words?"

" 'Thomas is cute.' That's what she said.

'Thomas is cute.' Are you coming or aren't you? I have to let her know."

"I'm coming."

"Wear your bathing suit. I'll come to your house and we'll walk. She said it. I'm not lying. She said it."

I said good-bye to Pettis and sat back with a satisfied smile on my face. Brigette thought I was cute. I was going swimming at her house. That wasn't half bad.

Then I remembered Elaine. I'd told her I'd call to see if she wanted to do something the next day.

What if she did? That would ruin everything. I'd miss going to Brigette's house. I might never be invited again.

I considered telling Elaine the truth but decided against it. I'd already upset her by telling her that no one had a high opinion of her. If I told her I wanted to see Brigette instead of her it would upset her more.

Then I thought, "Wait. It's good that she's upset. She's upset with me. It's going to take her a while to get over it. She probably won't want to see me tomorrow."

I sat up and called her. I didn't want to give her a chance to become less upset.

"Elaine," I said. "Do you remember I said something about getting together tomorrow? If you don't want—"

"I'd like to get together," Elaine said.

"You would? How come?" I was up and pacing. "I mean, it's not necessary. If you're busy or not up to it or something—"

"There's something I want to tell you."

"You're upset with me. I know that."

"I want to tell you something else," Elaine said.

"Tell me now," I said.

"I'd rather wait until we're together."

"Then I'll come to your house now. I'll be there in twenty minutes."

"No," Elaine said. "Let's wait until tomorrow."

What could I do? Tell the truth? The time for that had passed.

I thought fast and said that my mother wanted to tell me something. I put the phone to my side and wished that life were simpler.

"Elaine," I said after a moment, "my mother reminded me that my aunt Delores is visiting us tomorrow. I have to be here."

"Maybe we can get together before she comes," Elaine said. "What time is she coming?"

"Pretty early," I said.

"Can we get together after she leaves?"

"She usually stays pretty late."

"What about Sunday then?"

"Yeah, Sunday," I said. "We'll get together Sunday. You can tell me whatever you want on Sunday."

I shouldn't have done that," I thought, hanging up the phone. I only thought it a moment, though, then got excited again about going to Brigette's house.

We were there in the morning by eleven. It was a big house with a long driveway.

"Whatever you do, don't be uncouth," Pettis said, ringing the doorbell. "This isn't Krauss's house. You should've worn a different bathing suit. That one's a little loud. Hello, Mrs. Coates. How are you? This is Thomas Trible."

Brigette's mother had opened the door. She was wearing a white pants suit. After we said hello, she sent us through the house to the pool in the back.

"Not bad, is she?" Pettis said when she was behind us. "She always wears hoop earrings. She's thinking of streaking her hair. That's a new couch in the living room. It took forever to decide on a pattern."

The kitchen door led to a deck and the deck to the pool. Brigette, Francine Hart, and Priscilla Martin were standing near the edge.

"Hello, girls," Pettis said when we reached them. "I hope you were able to contain yourselves waiting for Thomas and me."

We said hello to one another and Brigette said, "We were about to go for a swim. Would you like to join us?"

"What do you say?" Pettis asked me.

"Not right now," I said.

"You girls go ahead," Pettis said. "We'll be available for mouth-to-mouth resuscitation."

The girls left us, and I said, "Pettis, your sense of humor."

"Never mind my sense of humor," he said. "Did you see how Brigette looked at you?"

"No, I didn't see how she looked at me."

"You had to see. Nobody could be that oblivious. What do you think of Francine? I think she has her eye on me."

$P$ettis and I reclined on chaise longues and watched the girls swim. He folded his arms on his chest, crossed his feet, and said, "Is this the life or isn't it?"

I was thinking about Elaine. I was feeling guilty about lying to her.

"Brigette is a fish," Pettis said as she swam past us. "I swear she's a fish."

I wondered what Elaine wanted to tell me.

"You don't think it's my imagination about Francine, do you?" Pettis said.

"I don't know."

"You do think she's cute, don't you?"

"Yeah, she's cute."

"Do you think Priscilla is cuter?"

"It's a tie."

Brigette climbed from the pool. She dried herself with a towel and sat on a chair at the other end of the pool from us.

"Now's your chance," Pettis said, sitting up and nudging me with his elbow.

"Now's my chance for what?"

"Now's your chance to talk to Brigette alone."

"Why should I?"

"That's what she wants. Why do you think she got out of the pool ahead of Francine and Priscilla? Why do you think she chose a chair with another chair next to it? Hurry, will you. You're wasting an opportunity. Go talk to her."

"All right. All right," I said. "Don't get excited. I'll talk to her."

Brigette smiled as I approached her. I asked if she minded if I sat down, and she told me to go ahead.

"You're a good swimmer," I said.

"Thank you," she said, running a comb through her hair.

"You have a nice house."

"I know. I don't have my own private bathroom. Some of my girl friends do. I wish

65

there was room for a tennis court. I can play at the club, but you have to go there and everything and sometimes the courts are occupied."

"I know what you mean."

"Do you play tennis?"

"No."

"I have about twenty tennis outfits."

"That's nice."

She quit stroking her hair and folded her legs.

"What do you like to do, Thomas?"

I mentioned riding my bike and reading Sherlock Holmes mysteries.

"I know Sherlock Holmes," Brigette said. "I saw a movie with him on television. It was about a dog."

"That's *The Hound of the Baskervilles*."

"I didn't like it. You could hardly understand everyone's English accent. And a lot of it was in the fog so you couldn't see."

"I saw a movie last week. It was about these two evil sisters and this priest. It was pretty good. It was French."

"Did it have subtitles?"

"Yeah."

"I hate subtitles," Brigette said, stroking her hair again. "We have to read so much at school. Who wants to read at the movies?"

Lunch was served on the deck. We were talking about school when Francine mentioned that the biographies were due Wednesday. Pettis told Brigette he hoped she was doing justice to the greatness of her subject.

Priscilla asked me what it was like having Elaine for a partner. Before I could answer, Brigette said, "How could you stand being in her house?"

I looked at her, wondering what she meant, and she said, "Alan said you said her house was disgusting."

I glared at Pettis.

"You said it was small and the paint was peeling," he said.

"That's not the same as saying it's disgusting, is it?" I said.

"Her father is a poet or something," Brigette said. "He wears a ponytail."

"Go away," Priscilla said.

"He does, doesn't he, Thomas?" Brigette said. I glared again at Pettis. "She calls him and her mother by their first names."

"Oh, God," Priscilla said. "My parents would kill me if I called them by their first names."

"That's because," Brigette said, "your parents are normal."

"Elaine's parents . . ." I said in a loud voice, and everyone looked at me. "Elaine's parents . . . Elaine's parents are all right," I said more softly.

"Hello, Daddy," Brigette said. Her father had come out to the deck. He'd been away someplace all day.

"Hello, sweetheart. Hello, children," he said. "Are you all enjoying yourselves?"

"Yes," Brigette, Francine, and Priscilla said in unison.

"I'll put it this way, Mr. Coates," Pettis said. "I've had worse times in my life."

By then I was un-
happy with the company and unhappy with
myself for not saying more to defend Elaine.
Time to leave couldn't have come soon
enough.

"Your manners were decent at least," Pettis said on the way home. "You could've been
friendlier, though. What got into you toward
the end?"

"Why did you do it, Pettis?" I asked. "Why
did you do it?"

"Do what?"

"Repeat what I told you about Elaine. Why
did you do it?"

"You didn't tell me not to do it."

I told him if he were half intelligent he'd
have known, without me telling him, that I
didn't want him to do it. I told him to remind
me never to tell him anything in confidence
again. I told him, because he had it coming
to him, that big houses in snooty neighborhoods might impress him but didn't impress
me. I asked if it ever occurred to him that
Brigette was vain and spoiled and shallow.

He listened with a hurt expression on his face. We walked on in silence. Then he said, "Anyway, what did you think of the Porsche?"

I was at Elaine's house early the next morning. I wanted to hear what she had to tell me and I wanted to tell her, to smooth my conscience, that I'd gone to Brigette's house.

We sat on the porch steps. Elaine said that she missed seeing me the day before and I said that I missed seeing her.

I took a deep breath, getting ready to tell her about Brigette.

"Thomas," she said.

"What?"

"I don't have contempt for the others in our class. That's what I wanted to tell you." She was staring into my eyes. "I feel different, Thomas. My family is different and I'm different. They don't—I'm afraid they don't like me because of it.

"So I pretend not to care. It doesn't hurt as much that way. It would be much worse, Thomas, if they knew that I care."

I didn't know what to say. Elaine was still staring at me.

"They like you," I said finally.

"They don't," Elaine said. "You said yourself that they don't."

"I didn't mean—"

"You meant it, Thomas. You know that you meant it."

"They'd like you if you gave them the chance," I said.

"I can't change for them," Elaine said. "I'm the person that I am."

"You don't have to change," I said. "You have to let them know you. I know you and like you."

"But—"

"You are different, Elaine. That's not bad. It's good. It makes you interesting. Who else do I know who reads—what was that you were reading in the school yard when I came to make arrangements?"

"A short story by Tolstoy."

"Who else do I know who reads short stories by Tolstoy and meditates and goes to foreign movies?"

Elaine smiled with her lips. "Thank you for saying that, Thomas."

"It's true," I said.

"Our relationship has been important to me."

"Same here."

"I trust you and feel comfortable with you." She smiled again. "Come, Thomas. It's time for another walk."

Why did I lie?" I asked myself as we walked. "Why did I go to Brigette's house in the first place? Why did I lie?"

"I hope I didn't embarrass you," Elaine said.

"When?"

"What I said on the porch. Did it embarrass you?"

"No."

"Good. I'd never want to embarrass you."

"Why did I lie?" I asked myself again. "Look where it got me. Why did I lie?"

"Elaine."

"Yes, Thomas."

"Yesterday . . ."

"What, Thomas?"

"Nothing. I mean, did you go to the park yesterday?"

"Yes, Thomas. I read."

I couldn't tell her. Not so soon after she said she trusted me.

"Elaine."

"What is it, Thomas?"

"I'm not feeling that well."

"No, you don't seem yourself today," Elaine said. "Would you like to go back to my house?"

"I think I better go home," I said. "I probably need some rest or something."

Why did I lie?" I asked myself a hundred times more on the way home. I promised myself to tell Elaine the truth the next day and to begin to be a good friend to her.

"If Elaine calls," I told my mother—she was at the kitchen table having tea—"tell her I'm feeling better but I'm sleeping."

"Weren't you feeling well?" my mother asked.

"And tell her, if it's mentioned or anything, that Aunt Delores was here yesterday."

"Aunt Delores? Why in the world—"

"Tell her. That's all. Tell her."

"What is this about, Thomas?" my mother said. "You know how I feel about lying."

"This once," I said.

"Nothing good ever comes of it, Thomas."

"I know. I know," I said. "I'll never ask again. I'm going to my room. Please, this once."

The first thing in school in the morning I apologized to Elaine for cutting short our walk the day before and arranged another walk after school. I didn't care—I was glad—that there were people nearby to hear.

I walked with Elaine from class to class and sat with her in the lunchroom. Twice, my heart pounding, I was going to tell her I went to Brigette's house but couldn't bring myself to say the words.

I suggested, as we left school for the day, that we take our walk in my neighborhood. Elaine smiled and said that that wasn't necessary.

"Let's walk in my neighborhood for the sake of variety," I was saying when Brigette called my name from behind. Elaine and I stopped and waited for her to catch up to us.

"Thomas, I meant to tell you— Hello, Elaine," Brigette said.

"Hello," Elaine said.

"You left your towel at my house,

Thomas," Brigette said, and I felt myself grow weak. "Yours was blue and white, wasn't it?"

"I think so," I said and, taking Elaine by the sleeve, started away with her.

"Why is your towel at Brigette's house?" Elaine asked.

"I don't know. I probably left it there. Did we decide to walk in my neighborhood?"

"Why did you bring it there?"

"She invited me to go swimming. She has a pool. She invited Pettis and Francine and Priscilla too. It was a spur-of-the-moment idea. Come straight home with me."

"That was nice of her. She must have a nice house."

"It's all right. She doesn't have her own bathroom or anything. Call your father from my house and let him know where you are."

"When did you go?"

"What?"

"When did you go to Brigette's house?"

"When?"

"Yes, when?"

I stared in front of me. I looked at Elaine and stared straight ahead again. Then I told her.

"Saturday?" Elaine said. "Saturday your aunt—" Her eyes narrowed. "No, your aunt didn't visit you Saturday, did she?"

"No," I said hanging my head.

"You lied to me, didn't you?"

"Yes."

"Did you tell Brigette and the others how you lied to me?"

"No."

"Did it amuse them?"

"I didn't tell them."

"Did you tell them how pathetic I am?"

"No."

"Did you tell them that I'm desperate for their friendship?"

"No."

"What did you tell them?"

"Nothing."

"I don't believe you. Your face is betraying you. What did you tell them about me?"

"Hardly anything."

"What did you tell them? Tell me what you told them about me."

"We talked about your house being small. I once mentioned it to Pettis—"

"What else?"

"Nothing."

"What else?"

"Pettis told Brigette you call your parents by their first names. I'd told Pettis—"

"You were making fun of us," Elaine said.

"We weren't."

"You were."

"We weren't. I swear. We weren't."

Elaine told me to keep lying and I might get good at it. Then she hurried away.

I called as soon as I got home, but Elaine wouldn't come to the phone. Her father told me that she seemed upset and suggested that I call later.

During dinner my father told my mother he'd bought them opera tickets. My mother was surprised and excited.

My sister asked when she was going to get to see Elaine again. My father said that he wanted to see her, too.

I called Elaine after dinner. Her mother said that she was resting and didn't want to be disturbed.

"Will you give her a message for me?"

"Yes."

"Tell her— Nothing. I'll tell her when I see her."

When I saw her at school in the morning, she wouldn't even look at me. I waited until she was at a table alone in the lunchroom to try to speak to her.

"Elaine."

She was reading and didn't look up.

"I'm sorry, Elaine."

She still didn't look up. I returned to my seat. Pettis asked what Elaine's problem was and I didn't answer him.

I walked home alone, stayed in my room until dinner, and returned there right after. At nine o'clock I dragged myself to my desk to write Elaine's biography. Mrs. Montgomery had said that she'd accept no excuses for lateness.

The biographies seemed all anyone was talking about in school the next day. "Show me yours and I'll show you mine," everyone was saying.

Not Elaine and me. Elaine still wasn't even looking at me.

"I trust the biographies are all completed," Mrs. Montgomery said when we got to English. "Let's have a few read to the class before they're collected. Are there any volunteers?"

On an impulse I raised my hand. Then I was standing in front of the class. I glanced at Elaine staring at me from her desk by the window and began to read.

Sherlock Holmes said, "It's a capital mistake to theorize before you have all the evidence. It biases the judgment."

I formed an opinion of Elaine Moore before I really knew her. A lot of people do. I discovered that my opinion was all wrong.

Elaine was born and raised in Schenectady. She lives in a house and neighborhood that aren't that impressive, but she's content with them.

Her father is a poet and her mother is a social worker. Elaine calls them by their first names. They're both intelligent and kind and go out of their way to make someone feel comfortable.

Elaine has no brothers or sisters. Sometimes, when she's lonely, she wishes she did.

Elaine is very intelligent, too. She reads more than any person I know. Recently she's been reading short stories by Tolstoy. She's fond of Sherlock Holmes mysteries by Arthur Conan Doyle.

Elaine and her parents are vegetarians. Elaine is sometimes intolerant of those who aren't.

Elaine's family has no car. Elaine feels that cars are dangerous and ecologically disastrous and aesthetically offensive.

Elaine enjoys opera and knows a lot about it. She goes to foreign movies. She likes to read in the park and take walks.

She's generous and magnanimous.

She doesn't care too much about possessions.

She has a good sense of humor. It takes a while to get used to it. She's sarcastic sometimes but never tries to hurt anyone.

While I was learning about Elaine, I learned a lot about myself. Some of it wasn't that good. I'm going to try to be more like Elaine.

Elaine Moore has a lot of wonderful qualities. She's a great person and she's going to have a great life. If you get to be her friend, you're very fortunate.

It had been quiet while I read and stayed quiet while I returned to my seat.

"Thomas, that was lovely," Mrs. Montgomery said.

"Thank you."

"Good job," Pettis whispered from his desk behind mine.

"Was that the first time you heard your biography, Elaine?" Mrs. Montgomery asked.

Elaine didn't answer right away. All eyes were on her. She looked at me, then at Mrs. Montgomery again, then nodded and looked down at her desk.

I'd been home about an hour, lying on my bed brooding, when my mother came to my room. "You have company," she said. "Elaine is here."

"What?" I leaped from the bed.

"Shall I tell her to come in?"

"Yeah. I mean, no. What does she want? All right. Tell her to come in."

My mother left, and in a few seconds Elaine arrived. She stopped a few steps into the room. I was still standing by the bed.

"Hello Thomas."

"Hello."

"Am I intruding?"

"No."

She took another step. "I thought you might want to take a walk."

"Now?"

"We still haven't walked in your neighborhood."

I said that I had to put on my sneakers. Elaine said that she could wait. I sat down on the bed to do it.

"Thank you, Thomas."

"What?" I looked up from tying a sneaker. "Oh, yeah. You're welcome."

"It was kind of you."

"Did you like it?"

"I liked it very much."

"I wasn't sure. When you didn't say anything afterward—"

"I was speechless, Thomas. You left me speechless."

I finished with my sneakers and got up.

"I worked hard on it," I said as we left the room.

"I could tell," Elaine said.

"I got a lot of compliments."

"You deserved them."

"I meant all of it, Elaine."

"I know you did, Thomas."

We reached the front door. I called to my mother that we were leaving. She called back, "So long," from the kitchen.

"What did you think of the way I quoted Sherlock Holmes?" I asked as we descended the porch steps. "Wasn't it clever?"

"It was," Elaine said. "Wasn't that from *A Study in Scarlet*?"

<br>

M rs. Montgomery returned the biographies a few days later. Afterward Elaine and I returned to homeroom together.

"I got an A," I said.

"That's nice," Elaine said.

"What did you get?"

"An A."

"Mrs. Montgomery wrote on mine that she could tell it came from the heart."

"She wrote on mine that it was thoughtful and well written."

"Do you think I should read it?"

I was curious about what Elaine had written about me. When I'd asked, she'd said, "You'll see." That sounded ominous when I considered what had happened between us around the time she wrote it, and not sure I wanted to know, I hadn't asked again.

"Yes, you should read it," Elaine said, and handed it to me. I stood against the wall reading it while Elaine stood beside me.

"This isn't that bad," I said after a couple of paragraphs.

"I gave you the benefit of the doubt," Elaine said.

"It's pretty flattering," I said, continuing to read.

"I may have gotten carried away," Elaine said.

"I am pretty sensitive, aren't I?" I said.

"Perhaps I wrote it with someone else in mind."

"Am I really an innocent when it comes to the arts?"

"Oh, then I was thinking of you after all."

"Thank you, Elaine," I said when I'd finished reading.

"You're welcome, Thomas."

"You're a nice person, Elaine."

"I know, Thomas. I have so many wonderful qualities. You're fortunate to be my friend."

A few weeks have passed and it seems that everyone—Pettis and Francine and Priscilla and Krauss and Brigette included—is trying hard to be Elaine's friend. I asked her to go to the park with me today and she said she'd already accepted an invitation to Francine's house. It wasn't the first time she had other plans when I wanted to do something with her.

"You never have time for me anymore," I complained.

"I'm afraid I'm in demand," Elaine said.

"Don't get a swelled head," I said.

"I won't," she said. "I won't forget, Thomas, that I owe it all to you."

The last time we went to the park, while she was giving me another lesson about flowers, I told her that I'd been meditating. I'd have told her sooner if I hadn't been embarrassed about it.

"I took a book about it from the library," I said. "It's got this woman in leotards on the cover. I've been meditating every night. It's not that easy. You have to relax and everything. I think it's doing me some good, though. I don't twirl my hair as much, do I?"

Elaine said I didn't. She showed me her nails and asked if they looked better. I said that they did.

"Your hair looks good, too," I said.

"Thank you," she said.

It was in a braid. She often wears it in a braid these days. Pettis says that it shows off her cheekbones—Pettis is probably going to become a hairdresser or cosmetologist or something—and that that's the reason she looks so good that way.

WB
HG
JB